Gut

Suddenly, Craig fe

socking him in the guts.

'Ugghh,' he groaned, doubling over. He braced his arm against the side of the shower stall to keep himself upright.

Then the taste hit him.

It rose from the back of his throat, gagging him.

He coughed. Hard.

First he coughed up blood that dribbled, then poured thickly, out of his mouth.

Then he felt something else coming up. It slid over his blood-slick tongue and out between his bloody lips.

He looked past his nose and saw a slug-white head emerge from his mouth – followed by a long wormlike body.

Other X-Files books in this series

#1 The Calusari
#2 Eve
#3 Bad Sign
#4 Our Town
#5 Empathy
#6 Fresh Bones
#7 Control

Voyager

THE X FILES™

The Host

Novelization by Les Martin

Based on the television series
The X-Files created by
Chris Carter

Based on the teleplay
written by Chris Carter

HarperCollins*Publishers*

Voyager
An imprint of HarperCollins*Publishers*
77–85 Fulham Palace Road,
Hammersmith, London W6 8JB

This paperback edition 1997
9 8 7 6 5 4 3 2 1

First published in the USA by HarperTrophy
A division of HarperCollins*Publishers* 1997

ISBN 0 00 648331 3

Set in Goudy

Printed and bound in Great Britain by
Caledonian International Book Manufacturing Ltd, Glasgow

To Mike and Barbara

Chapter One

Dmitri Protemkin should have been a happy man. For as long as he could remember, he had wanted to go to sea. But his dream of riding the waves around the world turned out to be a nightmare.

Dmitri was the lowest-ranking engineer aboard an aging Russian cargo freighter. The ship was once called the *Lenin*. Then the Soviet Union fell apart, and the ship was renamed the *Liberty*. But the crew had their own name for her. They called her a floating garbage can.

Right now the *Liberty* was far from her home port of Vladivostok. Under stormy skies, she plowed through the dark Atlantic near the New Jersey coast. Dmitri could feel the ship bucking as she hit heavy swells. That was the only way he knew he was at sea. He lived belowdecks, slaving in the engine room, wolfing down greasy food in the galley, or sleeping like a log in his bunk. The last time he had seen the ocean was when he went topside to heave over the railing. At least by now he was no longer seasick. But still, life on the *Liberty* made his previous job as a sheep farmer look good. Dmitri was counting the days until the ship hit land and he could see trees and grass and smell fresh air again.

His shift for the day was almost over. Hauling a coil of rubber tubing, he climbed down an iron ladder to the smoke and din of the engine room. After he finished patching a leaky oil connection, he would be able to knock off.

He heard a voice booming over the engine noise, "Dmitri!"

Waiting for him was Serge Steklov, the ship's chief engineer. Serge's broad, bearded face wore a big smile.

Dmitri braced himself. He wondered what rotten new job Serge had for him.

"We have a pressing problem," Serge told him. "I have received a report that our toilets are backing up. We can do without our engines—but not our toilets. We must see what we can do."

Dmitri grimaced. Serge said "we." But he meant one person alone.

"Follow me," Serge said.

He led Dmitri back up the ladder, then through a narrow corridor to the bathroom that the entire crew except the officers used. There, the two of them sloshed through brown water that had overflowed from the toilets.

"The whole system seems to be backing up," Serge said. "We'll have to investigate."

They left the bathroom, and went down another ladder into the depths of the ship. There a couple of crew members were grabbing quick forbidden smokes.

Serge ignored them as he tapped a square of metal plating on the bulkhead. "Behind this is the toilet disposal tank," he said. "We must find and remove whatever is in there blocking the system."

"Why is this always my job?" Dmitri griped.

Serge gave a hearty laugh, his big belly shaking.

"Because you are young," he told Dmitri. "And because it is terrible, smelly work."

As the two sailors joined in his laughter, he handed Dmitri a pneumatic drill.

Grimly Dmitri set to work removing the bolts that held the metal plate in place.

After ten minutes of sweaty work, he removed the plate.

He was almost knocked over by the odor that wafted out.

Standing well away from the opening, Serge said, "Go on, Dmitri. Take the plunge."

Dmitri turned his face away from the opening, and inhaled deeply. He held that breath as he reached in with a flashlight and stuck his head into the tank.

He played the light around the rippling filth, looking for the blockage. He leaned farther in, hunting without success, until his air began to run out.

Suddenly, something reached out of the

muck. It grabbed him around the neck and yanked him face forward toward the reeking stew.

Without thinking, he took a deep breath of the putrid air, then screamed.

Serge and the two other crew members rushed forward to grab Dmitri's kicking legs as his head was pulled under. They were big men, strong men—but they were not big or strong enough to stop whatever it was they were up against.

Dmitri's body was ripped from their clutching hands and vanished through the opening.

The stench forgotten, Serge stuck his head into the tank, just in time to see the soles of Dmitri's workboots as they disappeared into the churning muck.

Then he saw a pale shape that made him jerk his head back and bellow to the bug-eyed sailors, "Flush the tanks! Flush the tanks!"

As they obeyed, he stared into the hole.

Only when he heard the roar of pumps emptying the storage tank into the sea did he breathe easier.

Chapter Two

FBI Special Agent Fox Mulder was sitting on a hard metal folding chair in the musty supply room of a motel in Washington, D.C. The headphones on his ears were connected to the listening device on the table in front of him.

With five hours still to go on his shift, he was halfway through his bag of sunflower seeds. A pile of shells lay on the table.

With his forefinger, he flicked a shell over the tabletop at an empty styrofoam coffee cup facing him.

Bingo. The shell went into the cup.

Mulder grimaced. That was the only thing he had accomplished today.

Then he went back to listening to a phone conversation that had started twenty minutes earlier.

The men on the phone were definitely up to no good.

But the worst part of it wasn't what they were planning. It was how boring their plans were.

"Drake says he can set it up, but the cost sounds a little rich," said one.

"Dave's a stand-up guy," said the other. "If he's putting it together, you'd be a fool to pass it up."

"I hear you," said the first. "I just—"

"You just what?" the second asked. "You want to take a dip, you got to test the water. You just don't want to get wet."

"No, man," said the first. "Dippage is sacred."

Mulder sighed, then yawned. The two men had been beating around the bush for nearly a week now, calling each other at least three times a day. People say that women like to talk on the phone. But nobody could beat criminals for flapping their jaws. By the time these wiseguys decided to actually make a move, Mulder would have retired from the FBI.

Or quit.

Or been fired.

Whichever came first.

Right now, Mulder wasn't sure if he cared which came first. Months earlier, the bureau had closed the X-files. Mulder's partner, Special Agent Dana Scully, had returned to Quantico. And Mulder had found himself assigned to a series of routine—and routinely boring—cases. He was starting to wonder if it was worth it.

"So I said to him—" the first voice was droning on, when Mulder saw the supply room door opening.

His hand went to his shoulder holster.

Then he relaxed and let his arm fall to his side.

The two men coming through the doorway flashed FBI badges. But they didn't need IDs. Their dark suits, white shirts, and poker faces were standard bureau issue.

"Agent Mulder?" asked one.

"Yeah," Mulder said, taking off his headphones to hear better.

"Agent Brisentine here," the man said.

"Glad to meet you," said Mulder. "But I don't really think I need backup. What I do need, though, is a good crossword puzzle. I finished the one in the paper in ten minutes."

"You are being relieved from your current assignment," Brisentine said.

"For too much caffeine on duty, I presume," said Mulder sarcastically.

Brisentine did not crack a smile. "Agent Brozoff will take over," he told Mulder. "You have a flight to catch."

"Where am I going?" Mulder asked.

"To investigate a murder," Brisentine said. "In Newark, New Jersey."

Agent Brozoff silently took the headphones from Mulder and put them on. When Mulder stood up, Brozoff sat down in the chair without missing a beat.

Mulder handed him the rest of his bag of sunflower seeds.

"Enjoy yourself," Mulder said, and followed Brisentine out of the supply room.

"You're flying out of National. Your contact

in Newark is a Detective Norman," Brisentine went on.

"How did I get this job?" Mulder asked.

"Assistant Director Skinner made the request," Brisentine said.

Mulder's brow furrowed. "You say Skinner requested me?"

"So I heard," Brisentine said.

Mulder shook his head, but said nothing. Ever since Skinner had told him that the X-files were being shut down, his relationship with the assistant director had gotten pretty tense. Now Skinner was requesting that he investigate a murder.

As Mulder followed Agent Brisentine down the hallway, he couldn't help but wonder: Was this new case a sign of hope for the X-files? Or an omen that things were going to get much, much worse?

Chapter Three

Mulder didn't have to wait long to find out. Less than an hour later, he stepped out of his rental car in downtown Newark.

As he did, a young man in a rumpled suit came to meet him. "Detective Norman?" Mulder asked.

The man nodded, and Mulder went on. "Special Agent Mulder, FBI," he said, flashing his ID. "Fill me in."

"Glad to," Norman replied. "My team has finished examining the corpse. I'll have them write up their findings."

"And the body itself?" Mulder asked.

"We've left him where we found him," said Norman. "He's all yours now."

"Thanks," said Mulder. "Can I have a look?"

"Be my guest," Norman said. He turned and called to a uniformed officer, "Kenny! Bring Special Agent Mulder here some footwear!"

The policeman came over carrying a pair of high rubber boots. Meanwhile, Norman stooped down and pulled on a pair of his own.

"What are these for?" asked Mulder, doing the same.

"Those are nice shoes you're wearing," Norman said. "You wouldn't want to ruin them."

Norman picked up a flashlight. Then he led Mulder over to the manhole and began making his way down the iron ladder.

At the bottom of the ladder were four uniformed policemen and another plainclothesman. They herded together as though they didn't want to be alone. All of them carried lit flashlights. Norman turned his on as soon as he stepped off the ladder.

The flashlights showed an eight-foot-high brick sewer tunnel. The brick looked as though it came from the last century.

Along the bottom of the tunnel ran a thick stream of raw waste.

Gingerly, Mulder stepped into it. The muck reached almost to the tops of his rubber boots.

Mulder followed as the policemen moved down the tunnel in a solid group. Their flashlights lit the filth flowing ahead of them.

"Watch yourself," Norman cautioned, as they waded forward.

"Yeah," said Mulder. "I wouldn't want to step in anything."

"Or fall in anything," Norman said. Then he added, "Get ready now."

But he was too late. Mulder had already inhaled. A blast of fresh stench hit him like a fist.

"They tell me it helps if you don't breathe through your mouth," Norman suggested.

"They lie," said Mulder.

"Don't they, though," said Norman, and his flashlight moved to where the smell came from. A body lay a few feet away, facedown and half submerged.

Mulder went to the body, then forced himself to squat and squint at the decaying corpse. Mulder may have seen uglier sights. But he couldn't remember when.

He stood up and asked Norman, "Who found it?"

"A sanitation worker," Norman said. "He was making a routine tunnel inspection. Otherwise, there's no telling when it would have been discovered. Not too many people strolling by down here."

"Time of death?" Mulder asked.

"All we can say is that it seems to have been down here a while," Norman said.

"Any ID?" Mulder asked.

"No," Norman said. "And we can't tell much from his face either. The front of the body is pretty much eaten away. You want us to turn him over?"

"No," said Mulder. "I'll take your word for it."

With that, Mulder turned away abruptly and started splashing back up the sewer tunnel toward the ladder.

"Hey!" Norman shouted after him.

Mulder kept going.

Norman tried again, shouting still louder, "Agent Mulder! What would you like us to do with the body?"

Mulder stopped and turned around briefly.

"Wrap it up and send it to the FBI!" he shouted back. "Care of Assistant Director Skinner!"

Chapter Four

Mulder's stomach was churning. But not with nausea anymore. Now it was with rage, as he glared at an office door at FBI Headquarters in Washington, D.C.

The nameplate on the door read: ASSISTANT DIRECTOR WALTER S. SKINNER.

Mulder opened the door and stormed in.

He looked at the desk where Skinner's secretary usually sat. Her chair was empty.

Mulder tapped his foot impatiently as he waited for her to appear.

He knew he wouldn't have to wait long.

A minute later the door to Skinner's private office opened, and his secretary came out. As always, she looked as cold and sharp as an icicle.

Mulder wasted no time being pleasant. He knew her just as well as she knew him. He cut to the chase. "I need to speak to him."

Her voice was as smooth as syrup laced with ground glass. "I'm sorry, Mr. Skinner is unavailable. If you'd like to have a seat."

The only move Mulder made was to step between the secretary and her desk.

"Will you tell him I'm here, please," Mulder said to her. "And that I need to speak to him. *Now*."

Her face told Mulder exactly what she thought of him in particular. And of anyone else who might defy her authority.

But she also heard the iron in his voice and recognized his determined stance. She could see how little chance she had of making him bend.

"One moment," she said.

She gave Mulder a glance to be sure he was not about to make an end run around her. Then she opened Skinner's door and leaned inside.

"Excuse me, Mr. Skinner," she said. "I'm very sorry to interrupt, but Agent Mulder is demanding to see you."

Through the open doorway Mulder saw Skinner, tall, bald, and tight-mouthed, glasses glinting, standing by his desk.

Skinner returned Mulder's cold look without blinking. Then he came to the doorway and said in a dust-dry voice, "Is there a problem, Agent Mulder?"

"Yeah, there is," Mulder said.

"Then make an appointment," Skinner said, and started to turn away.

Mulder's answer could have been shot out of a flamethrower. "It's kind of hard to make an appointment when you're up to your knees in raw sewage—and being jerked around from one meaningless case to another."

"Excuse me, I don't seem to follow you," Skinner responded, unmoved.

"What's my next punishment?" Mulder demanded. "Scrubbing bathroom floors with a toothbrush?"

"You're out of line, Agent Mulder," Skinner informed him.

"Really?" Mulder said, his voice still scorching. "I thought that was the whole point of these exercises in futility—to keep me in line. Or should I say, to put me in my proper place."

By now Mulder's heat was hitting home. Skinner's neck was turning red.

"Come into my office, Agent Mulder," Skinner snapped. "Please."

Mulder stepped past the secretary, who had been silently watching the exchange. As soon as Mulder was inside the private office, Skinner closed the door.

Only then did Mulder see the people sitting around the long conference table inside. The ones he recognized were high-level FBI brass. The ones he didn't looked even more important.

"Agent Mulder, please inform the room why you regard your homicide case in New Jersey as 'meaningless'," Skinner requested.

"It . . ." Mulder paused and swallowed. He felt all eyes on him. He felt their amusement, felt their scorn, as they waited for what he might say next. He went on warily. "It looks to me like a simple mob hit. Perhaps drug-related. Not the kind of case to waste FBI time or manpower on."

"Agent Mulder, consider your history at the bureau," said Skinner. "Consider how many of your cases have ended with less than satisfactory solutions—or any solutions at all."

"But—" Mulder began.

Skinner ignored him. "With your record, you are not one to judge what is or is not a waste of the bureau's time or manpower."

Mulder tried again to argue. "Sir, my work on the X-files was a very special kind of—"

Again Skinner cut him off. "The X-files were closed, Agent Mulder, for the reasons I have just mentioned. You will carry out your new assignments without hesitation. You will investigate them to the best of your ability. Is that clear?"

"Yes," was Mulder's muttered answer.

"I am looking forward to your field reports on the Newark homicide case," Skinner said. "Now, unless you have anything more to say, I suggest you get back to work."

Without a word, Mulder turned and left the room. He had run out of things to say. Now he could only wonder what he should do next.

Chapter Five

Mulder sat on a park bench on the bank of the Potomac. Ripples on the river reflected lights from the shore. Across the water was the brightly illuminated Washington Monument. It pointed toward the sky like a giant finger.

Mulder was not looking at that shining beacon, though. Nor was he looking at the stars above.

He sat with shoulders slumped, staring at the ground, and seeing nothing. Nothing in his present. Nothing in his future.

Suddenly he heard a voice behind him.

"Is this seat taken?"

He did not have to look up to know who had spoken. After teaming so closely and so long with Special Agent Scully, he knew her voice as well as he knew his own.

Still staring at the ground, Mulder said, "The seat is free. But I should warn you, I'm having violent impulses."

"Well, fortunately I'm armed," said Scully. "I'll take my chances."

A ghost of a smile crossed Mulder's face—a ghost from their days of give-and-take together.

"Be my guest," said Mulder.

Scully sat down beside him. But he still did not look at her.

"I hear you were a big hit with Skinner today," she said.

"Oh, yeah," Mulder said, and finally looked at Scully.

He saw the worry on her face. It was him she was worried about. *Well,* he thought, *she isn't the only one.*

"What did you hear?" he asked her.

"That you embarrassed him," Scully said. "And you didn't exactly win brownie points from the bureau directors, either."

Mulder shrugged. "Skinner was pushing me," he said. "So I pushed back."

"Sounds like your timing was off," Scully commented.

"Yeah, maybe," he said, staring into the dark. "But what does it matter? Why worry about timing when your time is up?"

"What are you trying to say?" Scully asked sharply.

"I don't know, Scully," he said. "I guess you reach a point where you can't just grin and bear it anymore."

"It shouldn't have come as a surprise," said Scully. "If you don't play by the rules, you pay the penalty. It's not like you ever tried to fit into the program."

"Yeah, I've been thinking about that," said Mulder. "Thinking about it a lot." He paused, then found the word for what he had been pondering. "I've been thinking about leaving."

Scully swallowed hard before she could answer. She had trouble saying the word as well. "Leaving? The bureau?"

Mulder said nothing. He didn't have to.

"Mulder, I think you're taking all this too hard," she said, searching for the right words.

"The bureau needs you."

"For what?" he demanded. "To slog through sewers? To yawn though wiretaps?"

"That's between you and Skinner," Scully said. "I'm sure you can work out something with him—if you do it the right way."

"Not after today."

"But what would you do if you . . . ?" Scully couldn't bring herself to finish the sentence.

Mulder jumped in. "I don't know," he told her. "Try to pursue my investigation of the paranormal somehow. There has to be a way."

"Look," said Scully, with more than a hint of desperation. "Request a transfer. Come back to the Behavioral Sciences Unit. I'm there now, and we can—"

"They don't want us working together, Scully." He wasn't arguing with her. He was simply telling her what they both knew. "And right now, that is the only reason I can think of to stay."

Scully was touched. Mulder had never been one to express his emotions. It was sad that his true feelings had come out so late.

Even sadder that it might be *too* late.

Scully saw the emptiness in his eyes. She tried to light a spark.

"What about this case you're working on?" she asked.

"It's a zero. Some two-bit hood, rubbed out bargain-basement style."

"Where's the body?" Scully pressed him.

Mulder shrugged. "It's been transferred to the FBI lab for final determination of the cause of death," he said. Then he looked at Scully and shook his head. "Look, Scully, I know what you're thinking and—"

"I can ask to do the autopsy," Scully broke in. "I believe my request will be honored. I'm one of the most qualified people they have."

"It would be a waste of your time," Mulder said. "There's nothing to this case. Skinner put me on it to rub my nose in it."

"You mean to tell me a dead body is nothing?" Scully asked.

"You don't believe me?" Mulder replied. "Okay, find out for yourself."

Scully heard the listless tone of his voice,

and realized Mulder was even further down than she'd thought. He wouldn't even rise to an argument.

She herself tried to keep her words from sounding as hollow as they felt. "I intend to do just that."

Chapter Six

It was easy for Scully to get the job of examining the corpse from the sewer.

All she had to do was ask.

When she unzipped the black body bag in the autopsy room, she saw why nobody minded her grabbing the assignment.

Or rather, she smelled why.

A white lab coat protected her suit. Latex gloves protected her hands. Big plastic goggles protected her eyes. But there was nothing to stop the stench from going straight into her nose—and then to her stomach.

"Ugghh," she muttered, and stepped back until her stomach settled down.

Then she went to work.

She snapped on her tape recorder and read

into it from her notebook, "Examination and autopsy of John Doe number 101356. Case number DP112148. Special Agent Fox Mulder, Field Investigator."

Then she put down her notebook and took a good look at the body on the stainless steel table.

There were times Scully was thankful she had trained to be a doctor before she joined the FBI. Medical school had taught her to look at corpses as if they were problems to be solved. It had trained her to blank out the idea that they once were people who lived and breathed and thought and felt. She learned to view body parts as if they were parts of a machine, not rotting flesh and blood.

Right now Scully needed all of that training to get on with this job without gagging.

Still looking at the corpse, she said into her recorder, "Body is an adult male, in an advanced state of decay. It weighs a hundred and sixty-four pounds in death, and is sixty-nine inches long. Its skin is mottled and discolored after being submerged in a highly bacterial environment. The cause and time of death are unknown."

Then she noticed something on the corpse's right arm, below the elbow. She leaned closer. On the filthy, decaying skin she saw faint markings. She could barely make them out. They might be a tattoo of some sort. A girlfriend's name, perhaps. Or a gang insignia.

"Possible identifying mark on right forearm," she recorded, and made a mental note to check into it later.

Right now, though, she had more pressing work to do.

Her job at the moment wasn't to find out who the corpse was. She had to discover what killed him.

To do that, she had to dig deeper.

She took a scalpel from her instrument tray. With swift, sure strokes, she slit the front of the body open from chest to thighs. It was as easy for her as peeling a banana.

She inspected the mass of body tissue within.

"The body cavities appear normal," she recorded. "The interior organs are intact. Their decay matches the decay of the outside skin."

Scully shook her head. Nothing yet. She had to go deeper. She put down her scalpel and picked up a pair of clippers.

Snipping as if she were pruning branches from a tree, she cut away the bones of the rib cage to expose the body's vital parts.

"The condition of the heart and lungs is good," she recorded. "There are no signs of disease or breakdown through aging. I can conclude the victim was a young adult, probably in his twenties."

Scully reached in and put her fingers around the liver. She squeezed it gently, the same way she would test a peach to see if it was ripe.

"The liver shows some signs of hardening," she reported. "Possibly the result of too much alcohol. Other than that, there is nothing in the corpse to indicate cause of death."

Scully took up her scalpel again and made another cut.

Her eyes bulged behind her goggles.

"Oh my God," she gasped, forgetting the recorder was on.

Something slithered up out of the cut.

It looked like a head of some sort.

A flat, white, slimy head.

A head with a round, suckerlike hole for a mouth.

Scully couldn't tear her eyes off it. But her hand moved as if it had eyes of its own.

She let her scalpel drop, and grabbed a pair of forceps from her tray.

Using the forceps like pliers, she pinched the head before it could dart back to wherever it had come from.

Slowly, carefully, she pulled at it. Inch by inch, a slimy slug-white worm emerged from the incision.

Definitely not the kind of worm you'd use for bait, she thought, staring at the foot-long creature wiggling furiously in her grasp.

Still looking at it, she wondered what Mulder would say to this.

One thing was for sure—he no longer could say that this case was routine.

Chapter Seven

Craig Jackson and his partner, Pete Helms, stood beside an open manhole on a Newark street. Both men wore sanitation department gear: white hardhats, bright orange shirts, waterproof coveralls, and heavy workboots.

"It's now or never," Craig said, shrugging at Pete. He took a deep breath of fresh air, then led the way down the rusty metal ladder into the sewer.

Once inside, the men made their way along a wooden catwalk attached to the wall of a huge tunnel. They played their high-powered flashlights over the sewage flowing below.

"Uh-oh," said Craig. "Trouble."

His light illumined a wire mesh screen that filtered the sewage on its way to the sea. A jagged tree trunk was wedged in a hole in the mesh.

"Must've been that thunderstorm the other night," said Craig. "It washed all kinds of stuff into the system."

"Your turn," said Pete. "I did it last time."

"Okay, okay," Craig said. "You go topside and get a piece of thirty-gauge replacement screening and some baling wire."

After five years on the job, Craig didn't even wince as he entered the waist-high muck. He waded to the tree trunk. Grunting, he started to wrestle it out.

He could feel the sweat pouring under his clothes by the time he got it free. Cradling it in his arms, he waded back to the catwalk and reached up to put the tree trunk on it.

Suddenly he was jerked backward. The trunk fell onto the catwalk as he plunged into the sewage screaming.

The scream echoed through the tunnel even after his head went under.

At the foot of the ladder, Pete heard it, and came running back.

He arrived just in time to see Craig's thrashing upper body break the surface.

"Help!" Craig shouted.

"Here—grab it!" Pete shouted, as he pulled a coil of rope from his belt and threw an end to his partner.

But before Craig could get hold of it, he went under again.

Standing with the limp rope in his hand, Pete stared down at the stream.

"Craig! Craig! Where are you?" he shouted, without a hope his partner could hear him.

A moment later, though, a voice answered, "Here! Here!"

Craig had broken the surface of the sewage, and was halfway through the hole in the screen.

Desperately he held on to the wire mesh. He was fighting against the current pulling him into the next sewer chamber where the stream of waste turned into a swirling river.

Pete threw the rope again, and this time Craig managed to grab it.

Craig held on for dear life as Pete used every ounce of his strength to haul his partner out.

At last, Craig lay on the catwalk. He was gasping for air and writhing in pain. Between his gasps, moans came from his mouth.

"What's wrong, Craig?" Pete asked, bending over him. "What hurts?"

Still gasping and moaning, Craig sat up partway—and Pete saw what was wrong, what hurt.

There was a rip in the back of Craig's heavy shirt just above his waterproof coveralls.

Through the rip in Craig's shirt, Pete could see a crude circle of bleeding, mangled flesh.

"Oh my God, what could have done that?" Pete muttered, and peered into the sewage below. "What the heck is down there?"

He didn't even want to guess. He just knew one thing.

"I gotta get help," he told himself as he started running for the ladder.

Chapter Eight

Craig Jackson stared into a blinding light.

"Hey, Doc," he said, "it ain't my eye that got hurt."

"I'm just making sure everything is in good working order," Dr. Jo Zenzola told him. She kept shining her penlight into Craig's eye. Her other hand, with a latex glove on it, held his eyelid open. Squinting, the dark-haired physician saw that the pupil of the eye was reacting normally. She snapped off the light and let the eyelid fall back into place.

"No damage to your nervous system that I can see," she told Craig. "The only danger now is tetanus developing from your wound. I'll give you a shot to prevent it. Then you can change out of your hospital gown and go home and get a good night's sleep. No reason you can't go to work tomorrow. If you experience difficulties, come back and see me."

"I've had worse cuts and just used a Band-Aid," Craig said with a shrug. "I'd be happy if you just gave me something to get this taste outta my mouth. It tastes like rotten meat—only worse."

"Let me take a look," Dr. Zenzola said. "Open your mouth."

Craig obeyed, and the doctor shone her penlight inside.

"I don't see anything abnormal," she said. "Do you have trouble swallowing?"

His mouth still open, Craig shook his head and grunted, "Unh-uh."

Dr. Zenzola snapped off the penlight and reached into her lab coat.

"Here, take this," she said, pulling out a stick of spearmint gum and handing it to Craig.

When he looked at it doubtfully, she assured him, "Don't worry, the taste will go away."

"I sure hope so," said Craig, unwrapping

the gum and putting it into his mouth.

Dr. Zenzola paused when she heard the door to her office open. She turned and spotted a man in a dark suit standing in the doorway. "Pardon me for a moment," she said, turning back to Craig.

She left her patient and stepped over to the man. She checked his ID and said, "Glad to meet you, Agent Mulder."

"Good to meet you, Dr. Zenzola," Mulder said. "How did you get my name?"

"The Newark police told me you might want to be contacted about this accident," she told him. "I must confess, I was surprised that the FBI was involved with the city sewer system. Is there something going on here that I should know about?"

"I don't know," Mulder said. "Maybe you can tell me."

The doctor gave him the facts in short order. "The patient, Craig Jackson, is a sanitation worker. He claims he was attacked by something down in the sewer this morning."

Mulder showed a spark of interest.

"Attacked?" he asked. "By what?"

"We have not been able to determine that," the doctor told him. "At first, I thought it might be a story that Mr. Jackson cooked up. You know, to get disability pay. But my physical examination indicates he was telling the truth."

As she spoke, Dr. Zenzola went about filling a hypodermic needle with a tetanus shot.

"What did your examination find?" Mulder asked.

"He is in satisfactory health," Dr. Zenzola said. "I've given him a large dose of antibiotics, and we're watching him for hepatitis from the polluted liquids he ingested."

"And the evidence of an attack?" Mulder asked.

"He has a wound on his back," the doctor said.

"What kind of wound?" Mulder wanted to know.

"A rather bizarre one," Dr. Zenzola replied, shaking her head. "It might be a violent skin reaction to some kind of bacterial infection, but that seems unlikely. It looks more like a bite of some sort. All I can say for sure is that I've never seen anything quite like it."

"How did he get it?" Mulder asked.

"You can ask him yourself," Dr. Zenzola said.

She went to Craig with the needle in her hand. As he held out his arm, she said, "This is Agent Mulder of the FBI. He'd like to ask you a few questions."

"Sure, shoot," Craig said to Mulder, and winced as Dr. Zenzola stuck the needle in his arm.

"Any idea what attacked you?" Mulder asked.

"Not for sure," Craig said, grimacing as the doctor slowly pushed the plunger down. "But I've been thinking it might have been a python."

"A python?" Mulder echoed, smiling slightly.

"Or maybe a boa constrictor," said Craig, relaxing as the needle came out and Dr. Zenzola swabbed the spot with alcohol. "Don't laugh. You have no idea what kind of stuff people flush down the toilet. We found an alligator in the sewer a couple of years ago. It's a zoo down there."

"But you don't know exactly what it was," Mulder said.

"Whatever it was, it was strong as the devil, I'll tell you that," Craig said, shaking his head at the memory. "It clamped down on me like a vise. It was all I could do to break free. And it sure left its mark."

"May I see the wound?" Mulder asked.

"If you got a strong stomach," Craig said. "And if it's okay with the doc."

"No problem," Dr. Zenzola said, and pulled Craig's gown aside to expose his upper back.

Mulder looked at the wound. Freshly cleaned, it was clear as a picture drawn on the pale skin. An angry red welt formed a large O close to four inches in diameter. Just inside the welt were four puncture holes spaced evenly apart. And in the center was an even larger hole.

"As I said, it looks like a bite," Dr. Zenzola commented. "But I can't imagine anything making a bite like that."

"The bite pattern *is* unusual," Mulder agreed, looking at it more closely.

His eyes no longer showed boredom—not a bit.

Suddenly the cellular phone in his jacket pocket chirped, and his hand flew to it.

He pulled the phone out and said, "Mulder here."

Somehow he knew who would be on the other end.

This case had begun to take a new turn. A strange turn. A turn that might lead . . . who knew where?

Suddenly it felt just like old times—the times he thought were gone forever.

"Mulder, it's me," Scully said.

Chapter Nine

"What's up?" Mulder asked Scully. As he spoke, he moved away from Dr. Zenzola and Craig Jackson, and turned his back for privacy.

"I need to see you," Scully said urgently. "I've just finished the autopsy on that John Doe from the sewer. I found something I think you should know about."

"What?" asked Mulder.

"I can't say for sure," Scully said. "It seems to be some kind of parasite living in the body. I'm going to examine it more closely. I should be able to tell you more by the time you get here."

"I'm up in New Jersey now," Mulder said. "I'll be able to catch a shuttle flight down to Washington in an hour. I'll drive to the lab straight from the airport."

"Fine," Scully said. "I'll get to work right away."

"Bye," said Mulder.

"See you," said Scully, and hung up.

As Mulder put the phone into his pocket, he could still hear the excitement in Scully's voice. The excitement of the chase.

He smiled to himself. She had probably noted the same excitement in his voice as well.

Behind him he heard Craig say to the doctor, "When can I get out of here? I'd just like to go home."

Then his phone chirped again.

What could Scully have come up with already? he wondered.

He pulled out the phone and clicked it on.

"Yeah?" he said into the mouthpiece.

The voice he heard was not Scully's.

It was a man's voice. Deep as darkness.

"Mr. Mulder?" it said.

"Yes," Mulder said.

"I think you should know—you have a friend at the FBI," it said.

"Who is this?" Mulder demanded.

The answer was a click. And the sound of a dead line.

Over that, Mulder heard Dr. Zenzola say, "If you don't have any more questions, Agent Mulder, I'm going to release this man."

"No, he can go," Mulder said, putting the phone back in his pocket.

He had no more questions for Craig Jackson. Right now he had a much more pressing question.

The question stayed on his mind as he drove his rental car to the airport and boarded the Washington flight.

He looked unseeing out the window as the plane flew through the night. He played back the phone message in his head again and again:

"*You have a friend at the FBI.*"

Who was the deep, dark voice on the phone?

Where was he coming from and what did he want?

Mulder remembered another "friend" he once had.

A "friend" who made contact only when and how he wanted to, and fed Mulder tidbits of information like bait on a hook.

A "friend" who Mulder referred to as Deep Throat.

Deep Throat was dead now. He had died right before Mulder's eyes. Otherwise Mulder could not have been sure of his death. Deception had been Deep Throat's profession and his pride.

Deep Throat had gasped out three dying words to Mulder.

Words of advice like a life preserver thrown to a man in a sea of treacherous currents and ravenous sharks.

Mulder still clung to those words:

"Trust no one."

But there was one person Mulder did trust.

And he was going to see her now.

He knocked on the door of the lab before opening it.

"Close the door," Scully said.

Mulder quickly stepped into the lab, shutting the door behind him. "You mentioned that you have something interesting to show me."

"I do," Scully said. "But I have one little warning first."

"What's that?" Mulder asked.

"I hope you haven't eaten recently."

Chapter Ten

Scully opened a metal drawer and lifted out a large glass jar.

She set the jar down on a stainless steel lab table and stepped aside.

"Take a look," she told Mulder.

He peered into the jar. It was filled with clear liquid. In the liquid floated a coiled white worm. It was nearly a foot long.

"Cute little thing," Mulder said. "Have you named it yet?"

"The textbooks call it turbellaria," Scully said. "More commonly, it's called a flatworm or a fluke."

Mulder gave it another look and said, "*This* was living inside the corpse?"

"Yeah," Scully said. "It looks like it had

attached itself to the bile duct and was feeding off the liver."

"Believe it or not, something like forty million people around the world are infected with parasite worms," she went on.

"Is this where you tell me some terrible story about what I can pick up from eating sushi?" Mulder asked. He continued to stare at the creature in the jar. It might have been dead, but floating in the liquid it seemed gruesomely close to being alive.

"Maybe you'd rather hear what you can catch from a nice bloody rare steak," said Scully.

Mulder finally looked away from the worm and asked, "So what does this have to do with solving the death?"

"Flukeworms like this one are very common in unsanitary conditions," Scully said. "There's a very good chance that it entered the victim down in the sewer."

"Before or after he died?" Mulder asked.

"I don't know," Scully said. "But according

to all the medical texts I checked, it's unlikely that a single worm like this could have killed him."

"Perhaps he was in a weakened condition to start with," Mulder suggested. "Sick. Or old. Or seriously damaged by alcohol or drugs."

Scully shook her head. "The victim was a young man—and in apparent good health. That's the weird thing. Other than this small parasite, I have been able to find no possible cause of death."

Mulder thought a moment, then reached into his pocket.

As he did so, he asked, "How does this worm attach itself to its host?"

"It's got what's called a scolex," Scully said.

"Which is?" Mulder asked, as he pulled a photo from his pocket.

"A suckerlike mouth with four hooking spikes," Scully said.

"Something that would produce a bite like this?" Mulder asked, and handed Scully the photo.

Her mouth dropped open as she stared

at it. She gave it another look, then said, "Where did you get this?"

"A workman was attacked this morning by something in the same Newark sewer where the body was found," Mulder said. "This is a photo of the wound on his back."

"And you're asking me if this is from a flukeworm?" asked Scully with amazement.

"Could it be?" Mulder wanted to know.

"I'm afraid you have to get real, Mulder," Scully said, trying not to smile. "The flukeworm has a tiny little mouth. This is a huge bite mark."

"How big can these worms get?" Mulder persisted.

"How big can these—" Scully started to say, then stopped as she realized what he was asking. She shook her head in disbelief. "Mulder, you will never change. It feels like old times working with you again."

Mulder smiled and nodded.

Then their smiles disappeared as they looked at the worm again.

"So tell me more about this worm," he said.

"This flukeworm is what they call an obligate endoparasite," Scully reeled off. "They live inside the host body. They enter the body when the host eats or drinks something containing their eggs or larvae. They are unpleasant little organisms and quite harmful to the health. But they are not, I repeat, *not*, creatures who go around taking huge bites out of people."

"That's good," Mulder said. "Because I don't want to have to report to Assistant Director Skinner that my murder suspect is a giant bloodsucking worm."

He picked up the jar, and said in a weary voice, "Well, that's that. Thanks for your trouble, Scully."

Scully laid a hand on his shoulder. "Sorry, Mulder. I really thought that there might have been something there. I wish there were."

"Yeah," Mulder said in a sarcastic tone. "Well, I'm sure this will be of interest to the Newark Sanitation Department at least. Maybe they'll launch an anti-parasite campaign."

Mulder paused for a moment. When he

spoke again, his tone was serious. “Look, Scully, I don’t know who you told about our conversation the other night. But I’d prefer it if you didn’t try to launch a campaign in the bureau on my behalf.”

“Excuse me?” asked Scully, puzzled.

“I don’t know who you talked to—” Mulder repeated.

“I didn’t talk to anyone,” she assured him.

“Well, somebody called and told me I had a friend at the FBI.”

“Who called you?” Scully asked.

“He didn’t choose to say.”

“Look, I don’t know what to tell you,” Scully said. “Except one thing. I wouldn’t betray a confidence.”

“Yeah,” said Mulder. “Of course you wouldn’t. Well, thanks for everything, Scully. I’ll see you.”

Chapter Eleven

"Those doctors don't know anything," Craig Jackson muttered to himself. "Easy for that Zenzola to say this taste is just gonna go away. She doesn't have to live with it."

Craig was standing in his bathroom, looking in the mirror. He had already checked out his wound—it still looked big and raw. He'd have to bandage it up again after he took a shower. Now he inspected his face. It didn't look much prettier than his back. It was drawn and pale, with a touch of green around the gills. Not that he ever got much of a tan, he thought, working down in the sewer tunnels day in and day out.

Craig put some fresh toothpaste on his brush. Maybe the third time he brushed his teeth would be the charm. Why wouldn't that lousy taste go away?

Craig opened his mouth and brushed as hard as he could. Then he took the brush out and swished the toothpaste around in his mouth before he spat it into the sink. He looked down at it and saw he must have brushed too hard. Red blood streaked the white froth. He looked in the mirror. He must have done a number on his gums while trying to scrub that taste away. Blood covered his lips.

He tried to take his mind off it. He tried to think positive.

Determined to put it all behind him, Craig stepped into the shower stall. He turned on the water hot and hard. It was his second shower of the day, but with the kind of work he did, you couldn't take too many showers. Somehow, they never totally did the job. Still, he'd have to do the best he could.

As the steaming water poured over him, Craig suddenly stopped thinking about the bad taste in his mouth.

He felt as though something was socking him in the guts.

Not from the outside, though. From the inside.

"Ugghh," he groaned, doubling over. He braced his arm against the side of the stall to keep himself upright.

Then the taste hit him again.

It rose from the back of his throat, gagging him.

He coughed—hard. It felt like he was coughing his lungs out.

But it was even worse than that.

First he coughed up blood that dribbled, then poured thickly out of his mouth.

Then he felt something else coming up. It slid over his blood-slick tongue, and out between his bloody lips.

He looked past his nose and saw a slug-white head emerge from his mouth—followed by a long, wormlike body.

Swaying with disgust, Craig watched the worm drop from his mouth to the floor of the shower stall. It swirled in the bloody water, then slithered down the drain.

Chapter Twelve

"Welcome to Sewage Central, Agent Mulder," Ray Heintz said when Mulder introduced himself.

Ray was the foreman of Newark's sewage processing plant. He had been roasted by wisecracks from friends and family about his work ever since he had gotten the job.

"Nice place you have here," Mulder said, glancing around the control room of the plant. It was spiffy clean. The air was sweet. Computer screens on the walls told workers in gleaming white hardhats that the system was running smoothly. There was nothing to suggest that the system processed a vast pool of liquid waste. Held in concrete tanks, the raw sewage was treated with chemicals to kill off bacteria. Then it went on its way through a long stretch of pipes to the sea.

"It's a state-of-the art operation," said Ray. He was a short, wiry man with a dark beard and thick glasses. His voice was quick, whether cracking jokes or handing out information. "We utilize the latest technology. We have to, in order to keep up with the increasing load, or at least stay only a step behind. One of the problems, though, is that a big part of the system is quite old, built around the turn of the century."

Ray turned and grinned at a sanitation engineer going past them. The man was elderly, and moved slowly, in no hurry to go outside.

"Some of the sewers are real old, right, Charlie?" Ray said. "They go back as far as you do."

"Oh, yes, sir," Charlie answered as he hurried through the double doors.

"Tell me, what part of the system was I in when I viewed the body your men discovered?" Mulder asked.

"That would be one of the oldest sections," Ray told him. "Big eight-foot tunnels. None of that in our new lines," he went on. "All of them are concrete pipe, not many of them bigger than twenty-four inches."

"And all the sewage in the city comes through this plant?" Mulder asked.

"Five hundred and sixty thousand people a day call my office on the porcelain telephone," said Ray.

Mulder nodded, and opened his briefcase. He pulled out the glass jar he had carried away from Scully's lab.

He handed it to Ray, who squinted at the creature floating inside.

"You ever see one of these before?" Mulder asked.

"It looks like a big old worm," said Ray, still staring, fascinated.

"It's called a fluke," Mulder said. "It was living inside the body that they pulled out of the sewer."

Ray shrugged, handing back the jar. "It wouldn't surprise me," he said. "No telling what's been breeding down there the past hundred years."

x x x

In another section of the plant, Charlie Hobbs was making his rounds along the metal walkways between the vast expanse of treatment tanks. Charlie had worked at the plant for nearly twenty-five years. And every day, he made a full inspection of the tanks, checking to see that everything was running smoothly.

Charlie's head turned when he heard a splash in one of the tanks behind him. Zigzagging along the metal walkways, he made his way over to the enclosure. He was just in time to see something slip below the surface of the murky water.

Rushing over to a control panel, Charlie grabbed the emergency phone and punched in the number of the main control room.

"Ray here," the foreman said, snatching up the receiver. He listened for almost a full minute as the voice on the other end went on frantically.

"Okay, okay, Charlie. I'll be right there," he said. Then, turning to Mulder, he added, "It looks as though we've got something."

Chapter Thirteen

Ray and Mulder found Charlie standing on a walkway above one of the hundreds of square concrete tanks of raw sewage. The engineer was staring at the rippling muck as if he had never seen liquid waste before.

"I'm draining the tank," said Charlie.

"What exactly did you see?" Mulder asked him.

"Can't describe it," Charlie said, still looking. "Ain't no words to do it. None that I know, anyway. Never saw anything like it."

"But you're sure you saw something?" Mulder asked.

"There it is!" shouted Charlie.

The turbines whirred into action. Mulder watched the level of the sewage slowly drop.

He and Ray saw the shape emerging from

the lowering surface at the same time. It moved through the liquid waste as swiftly and smoothly as a fish through water, but it was no fish.

It broke the surface before going under again. It was a sight no one who saw it could ever forget.

It was gray-white and shimmering with slime. But still you might say it was human—almost.

From the back, its head and body and arms and legs looked human.

But its face told a different story.

It was a gray-white face in a head without hair or ears. It had no nose, and two big slits with glowing red eyes. It had a huge hole for a mouth.

Around the hole were lips seeking something to suck, with four sharp teeth designed to bite down and hold.

No, you couldn't call it human. Not human at all.

But—what *could* you call it?

x x x

Back at the FBI laboratory, Scully stared at a picture of that inhuman mouth on her computer screen.

She clicked her mouse to bring up pictures of other such mouths and more information from the data bank.

As she did so, she made notes on a pad of yellow legal paper, and spoke into her tape recorder:

"Turbellarian flatworms are free-living carnivorous scavengers," she reported. "That is to say, they feed on flesh and are capable of traveling considerable distances to hunt for it. They are usually less than three centimeters in length."

She brought up more data, then went on. "They are hermaphroditic, that is to say, both male and female in one body. Thus they are able to reproduce alone, without a partner. Many species move from host to host, seeking nourishment to survive."

Scully paused again, and brought up a

full-length image of a flukeworm. She was studying it when she heard the noise of paper crumpling.

It came from just outside the closed lab door.

"What the—" she muttered to herself. Then she called out, "Who's there?"

No answer.

She was about to turn back to her work when she saw a corner of paper poking in under the door.

She went to the door, opened it, and looked down. A tabloid newspaper lay at her feet.

She stuck her head into the corridor and looked to her right and left. There was not a soul in sight.

Frowning, she stooped over and picked up the paper. She closed the door and locked it behind her, then took the paper over to her workstation.

The paper was one that usually featured front-page headlines about kidnappings on flying saucers or John F. Kennedy alive in a secret asylum or Elvis showing up at a party.

This issue had a big picture spread about live dinosaurs in the heart of Africa.

Scully scanned that story and found nothing but clearly doctored photos and demented eyewitness accounts. Still puzzled, she thumbed through the rest of the paper.

She stopped on page 5.

It was not the picture of a cargo ship with a Russian flag that had caught her eye.

Or the headline that read: "BIZARRE ACCIDENT ON RUSSIAN CARGO SHIP HAS OFFICIALS SUSPICIOUS."

It was the smaller headline below: "CREWMEN CLAIM CREATURE ATTACKED SHIPMATE IN SEWAGE HOLDING TANK."

She read the entire story once fast, then a second time more slowly.

Putting the paper down, she turned to her computer and clicked the mouse once, then twice, then a third time.

A picture of the corpse found in the sewer appeared. Then a close-up of its upper torso. Then a further close-up of its arm.

She clicked the mouse again. And again.

The markings on the arm became clearer.

A tattoo, she decided. Definitely a tattoo.

She zeroed in closer on the tattoo.

Some kind of letters. Strange letters.

Letters that could form a word.

She was still trying to figure out what they spelled when her phone rang.

She grimaced at the interruption, then picked it up.

"Scully," she answered.

"It's me," said Mulder's voice.

"Where are you?" Scully asked.

"At the Middlesex County Psychiatric Hospital in New Jersey," Mulder told her.

"Are you all right?" she asked.

"Don't worry, I haven't flipped out— despite what you may think when you hear what I have to tell you," Mulder said. Then he went on. "You know that fluke you found in the sewer corpse?"

"Yeah?" Scully responded.

"It must have been the runt of the litter," Mulder said.

"What are you talking about?" she wanted to know.

"I can't begin to describe it," he said. "You'd better get up here and see for yourself."

Chapter Fourteen

Mulder met Scully at the front desk of the hospital. After showing their badges, he led her past two armed policemen and down a long corridor lined with heavy metal doors. All of them had thick glass windows at eye level.

Mulder stopped in front of the last door. He motioned for Scully to take a look through the window.

"I don't see it," she said. Mulder leaned forward to take a closer look.

"There it is, tucked away in the far corner behind the pipes," he told her, poining toward a shadowy area of the cell.

"Oh my God," she said.

The lighting inside was dim, but still Scully could make out the naked creature crouched in the far corner of the bare room. The slime on its hairless gray-white skin gleamed in the low light. Its muscles bulged with strength. Its red eyes darted around in their slits, desperately searching for an escape they could not find. The lips of the huge hole in the middle of its face made sucking motions like a baby pleading for a bottle. But there was nothing babylike about the hooked fangs behind those lips.

"Is it male or female?" Scully asked, still at the window.

"Neither—or else both," Mulder said.

Finally Scully took her eyes from the glass.

"That fits," she said to Mulder. "Platyhelminthes, or parasitic worms, are often hermaphroditic." Then she added, "This is amazing, Mulder. The facial features of this creature are that of a parasitic worm—but expanded a hundred times. Yet its body is that of a primate—an ape, or a gorilla, or even a human being."

"That seems to sum it up," Mulder agreed.

"But where on Earth did it come from?" she wondered.

"I don't know," said Mulder dryly. "But it looks like I'm going to have to tell Assistant Director Skinner that the suspect is a blood-sucking worm after all."

Scully didn't smile at his joke, though. She was too busy with the flood of thoughts that ran through her head.

"Its mouth does look like it could have caused the wound in the photo you showed me," she said. "The wound on the back of that sewer worker—what was his name?"

"Craig Jackson," said Mulder.

"We'll have to follow up on that," said Scully. "Examine him more closely. Run some tests on him."

"I think we can be sure they'll confirm that whatever this creature may be, it caused that wound," said Mulder. "But we're still missing one important piece of information. The identity of the body found in the sewer."

"He was a Russian," Scully stated matter-of-factly. "A Russian named Dmitri."

"How do you know?" Mulder asked.

"He had a series of marks on his forearm—

a tattoo," she said. "They didn't seem to mean anything until I realized they were Cyrillic letters."

Scully reached into her briefcase and pulled out a computer photo of the tattooed arm. Then close-ups of the tattoo markings.

"Right, the Russian alphabet," said Mulder, after a glance at it. "Good work. But we still have to find out who he was. There must be about a million Dmitris in Russia."

"His full name was Dmitri Protemkin, and he was an engineer on a cargo freighter," said Scully.

"How do you know that?" Mulder asked.

"The information came from this," Scully said. She pulled the supermarket tabloid from her briefcase and handed it to Mulder, opened to page 5. "Somebody pushed this under the door of the lab."

Scully saw Mulder's eyes widen, and she gave him a long look before she said, "I guess you really *do* have a friend at the FBI."

Mulder gave her a smile in return—a grim smile.

Scully put her hand on his arm.

It was hard to find the right words for what she had to say, but she wanted too much to say it not to try.

"Mulder, when you go to see Skinner to turn in your field report and discuss your situation with him, I hope—" Scully hesitated, then went on. "I hope you know I'd consider it more than a professional loss if you chose to leave."

Mulder looked at his partner for a moment.

Then he turned to look at the creature once more.

It was still in the same corner, but it had huddled deeper into the shadows.

As though it were looking for a place to hide.

Chapter Fifteen

At nine the next morning, Mulder entered Assistant Director Skinner's office. Skinner was sitting behind his desk, flipping through Mulder's report.

"Sit down, Agent Mulder," he said.

Skinner set the report in front of him and said, "Everything looks in order. Quite satisfactory."

Mulder stared at Skinner, dumbfounded.

Skinner raised his eyebrows. "Something wrong, Agent Mulder?" he asked.

Mulder forced himself to keep his voice calm. "Wrong? No, sir. I'm just a little . . . surprised."

"Surprised?" Skinner echoed.

"Your response to my report is rather unexpected, considering the bizarre nature of the crime," said Mulder. "Not to mention the nature of the suspect."

"I am entirely aware of the strangeness of the criminal and of the crime," Skinner said. "The details were made extremely clear to me this morning when I spoke to the federal prosecutor about how to deal with the prisoner. But this meeting with you now has nothing to do with any of that. It is merely to give a final review of your work."

"You mean, I'm off the case now?" Mulder asked.

"The investigation is over," Skinner announced.

"When will the suspect be tried?" asked Mulder.

"No court date has been set," Skinner said. "We have requested that the suspect be given a full psychiatric evaluation to see whether the suspect is fit to stand trial. The suspect will be transferred to the proper facility for that examination."

"Psychiatric evaluation? Fit to stand trial?" Mulder repeated. "You know what the results will be. The suspect is not a man. It's a monster. You can't put it in an institution."

"What *do* you do with it, Agent Mulder?" Skinner asked sharply. "Put it in a zoo? It's already killed two people."

"Two?" Mulder asked.

"The sanitation worker who was attacked was found dead in his home as a result of his injuries," Skinner said.

"Craig Jackson?" Mulder asked.

"I believe that was victim's name," Skinner said.

Mulder stared at his report lying on the desk. It already looked lost there among all the others.

Bitterly he said, "You know, you once had a pair of agents who could have handled a case like this from the start. Agent Scully and I might have been able to save that man's life. But you shut us down."

Skinner met Mulder's accusing stare and held it with his own unblinking gaze.

There was a long moment of silence.

Then Skinner replied, "I know. This case

should have been an X-file."

There was another silence as Mulder looked at Skinner as if he had never seen the assistant director before.

Then Skinner continued, "We all take our orders from someone. That will be all, Agent Mulder," he added, dismissing him.

Chapter Sixteen

"Orders are orders," said Tom Mullins to Rick Foster.

"Yeah, and a job is a job," Rick agreed.

"Still, there should be limits," Tom said.

Tom and Rick wore midnight-blue nylon windbreakers with U.S. MARSHAL printed across the back. In their careers, they had done and seen a great many unpleasant things without flinching. But right now neither man wanted to look at the creature tied down on the rolling table they were wheeling down the corridor of Middlesex Psychiatric Hospital. The creature's body was covered in a sheet, but the head was exposed. One look at that head had been enough.

"Think it's human?" Tom wondered.

"Let's hope it's not—for our sake as well as its own," said Rick.

They wheeled the table past a cop at the corridor entrance. They went out an exit leading to a garage behind the institution. There a red-and-white transport van was waiting. On its rear doors was the Great Seal of the United States. EMERGENCY was printed in large letters along both sides of the vehicle.

"All yours now, Roger," Tom said to the man in the driver's seat, who wore a marshal's jacket as well.

"Load him on and I'll be on my way," Roger said.

Tom and Rick lifted the table into the back of the van and locked the wheels. Then they climbed out and locked the rear doors.

Tom gave the back of the van a loud slam with his palm, and the truck started up with a roar.

Watching the van drive away, Tom said, "Looks like he's in a hurry to make his delivery."

"I can't say I blame him," Rick observed.

Driving through the night, Roger kept his eyes on the empty highway ahead. Now and then he glanced at the speedometer to make sure he wasn't pushing the speed limit too hard. The last thing he wanted was to be pulled over by a state trooper and be asked about his cargo.

Another thing he did not want to do was turn and look through the window behind his head. He'd just as soon not see what lay tied down on the table.

He reached for the dashboard and snapped on the light in the rear compartment. He braced himself, turned, and peered through the window.

His stomach flipped over.

The table was bare. The restraining straps lay empty.

Roger braked to a screeching stop on the shoulder of the road. He grabbed his radio mike and barked, "This is vehicle forty niner forty. On Route 75, approximately ten miles north of Middlesex Psychiatric Hospital."

Then Roger raised his voice to say, "I am

requesting immediate backup and assistance. I repeat, *immediate*."

"Request received," a voice crackled over the radio. "Help is on the way."

Roger put down the radio, and picked up a shotgun from the seat beside him. He slid the firing bolt up and down to the ready position.

As Roger stepped out of the van, he glanced up at a sign that identified the spot as the Lake Betty Campground. The red neon of the sign cast an eerie glow over the area.

Holding his weapon in both hands, he made his way to the rear of the van. You could never be too careful.

But you could be too late.

One of the van's rear double doors hung half open. Some kind of tremendous force had hit it from the inside, springing the lock.

It could be out there in the night already—but it also might not.

Roger had to make sure.

His finger on the trigger, he used the shotgun barrel to open the door fully.

Gingerly he climbed inside.

The table still was bare. As far as he could see, the rear compartment was empty.

With one hand still on the trigger, he used the other to lift one of the limp leather straps that had held the creature to the table. It was covered with thick slime. Roger nodded. The straps had not been designed to hold anything that slippery.

Wiping his hand on his trouser leg, he ran his eyes over the shelves holding medical supplies.

Not that such a large creature could hide in such small spaces, but Roger was a thorough man.

Next he looked under a bench along one side of the compartment.

As he expected, nothing was there.

As he turned to look under the bench on the other side, his mind was already planning his moves after he finished up here.

That was as far as he got—before a pair of arms closed around him from behind like a vise.

Before a mouth fastened onto his back like a suction cup and four fangs bit into him like plunging knives.

Before his shotgun exploded into empty air and its echoes were drowned out by his screams.

Chapter Seventeen

"I called you as soon as I learned the details of the case," Police Detective Lieutenant Norman told Mulder.

Norman and Mulder stood beside the neon sign advertising "Lake Betty—Nature's Playground—Live Bait—Campsites Available Year Round."

The neon was turned off now, with the morning sun well clear of the horizon. The sun shone on the fields, the lakeshore, and the van parked haphazardly on the shoulder of the highway.

Parked near the van were four local police squad cars and two U.S. government vehicles. A swarm of cops and federal marshals fanned out from both sides of the highway, snapping photos and combing the area.

Mulder watched as a tanker truck bearing the name Sweetwater Sanitary Maintenance roared by them on the highway. Then he turned to Detective Norman.

"What have you got so far?" he asked.

"Well, we've got a dead marshal and an escaped prisoner," Norman said. "Other than that, we've got *bupkis*. If you don't know the local lingo, that means zilch, zero, not a clue. Any suggestions, Agent Mulder?" Norman asked.

"I'd watch all the storm drains, and any other access to the sewer system," Mulder said. "I have a feeling it's going to try to get back underground."

Norman grimaced. "What the devil *is* this thing, Agent Mulder?" he demanded.

"I'm not sure, but I think—" Mulder began, when the phone in his pocket chirped.

"Pardon me a moment," Mulder told Norman, as he took the phone out. He moved away a few feet for privacy, and said into the phone, "Mulder."

He recognized the voice on the other end.

The voice of the mysterious man who had called and told him he had a friend at the FBI.

"Mr. Mulder, I'll make this brief. Success in your current assignment is imperative. Absolutely essential."

"Who am I speaking to?" Mulder asked.

Mulder could hear anger simmering in the answer: "I am not here to answer questions. Do you hear me, Mr. Mulder?"

"Yes," he said. "Why is bringing this case to a satisfactory conclusion so essential?"

"It must be made undeniably clear that the X-files should be opened again," the voice said.

There was a click and the buzz of a dead line.

Mulder put the phone back in his pocket. He would have liked to think about the call. Sort through the possibilities of whom the voice belonged to.

But there was no time—not when Norman's walkie-talkie squawked again.

"Unit six four, copy," a voice told Norman.

"Six four, I read you," Norman responded.

"We're at a campsite roughly a quarter of a mile from your position," the voice said. "Our dogs tracked a scent from the van to a chemical toilet here. We thought the prisoner might be hiding inside, but it's empty."

Suddenly Mulder interrupted the conversation. "That's it," he said.

"Hold on, six four," Norman said, and looked at Mulder.

"The tanker truck," Mulder said, excitement in his voice. "What if it's on the tanker truck?"

Norman nodded, light dawning.

Chapter Eighteen

Mulder got into his car. Before he turned on the ignition, he made a few quick phone calls.

The Sweetwater Sanitary Toilet Maintenance Company told him that their trucks dumped their loads at the Newark sewage treatment plant. But there was no way to contact the drivers while they still were out on their routes.

Mulder tried to reach Ray Heintz at the treatment plant, but only got the foreman's answering machine. All Mulder could do was leave a request to keep a lookout for Sweetwater deliveries.

Ray Heintz gave Mulder a cheerful hello when Mulder arrived at the plant.

"The company that owns the truck you're

looking for doesn't keep detailed records. They had about five trucks in the area of Lake Betty this morning," Ray told him. "Three of them have already deposited their loads."

"So the truck in question could have come and gone," Mulder said.

"If it hasn't been here, it will be," Ray said.

"You're sure every truck dumps its load here?" Mulder asked.

"It's a state law," Ray said.

"And everything is processed through this plant?" Mulder asked.

"Yep."

"What happens to it after it's processed?"

"It empties through an outlet pipe five miles out to sea," Ray told him.

"Remember that creature we found in here a couple of days ago?" Mulder asked.

"It's not anything I'm gonna forget in a hurry—much as I'd like to," Ray said.

"Could it escape through that outlet pipe?" Mulder asked.

"Not likely," Ray said. "The system is full of filters and screens. Nothing much bigger than your little finger is gonna get through. If it's here, it will be trapped in one of the treatment tanks."

"So all we can do is wait for it to surface?" Mulder asked.

"Well, we can take a look around and see if we spot it," Ray told him.

For the next two hours, Mulder, along with Ray, Charlie, and four other sanitation engineers, walked metal grids separating the tanks of waste.

Mulder was nearly cross-eyed when the cell phone in his pocket sounded.

"It's me," Scully said. "Where are you?"

"At the sewage treatment plant in Newark," Mulder said. "I was playing a hunch that our friend might have gotten back into the sewer system."

"How?" asked Scully.

"Forget it," Mulder said. "It was stupid. I've wasted a lot of time here—and I don't like to think where the creature may be now. Maybe the lake. Maybe anywhere. We can only be sure that it's on the loose."

"Well, then, you're not going to like what I have to tell you," Scully said.

"What do you mean?" Mulder asked.

"It didn't occur to me at the time, but I think that worm I found in the body was an incubating larva," she said.

"A larva—you mean, an early-stage life-form?" asked Mulder, trying to digest the information. "A life-form that can grow into—"

"Into the full-grown creature we saw," Scully confirmed. "That creature, whatever it is, is transmitting eggs or larvae through its bite. It's planting them in the people it attacks. That explains the hole in the center of the wound on the sanitation worker's back."

"The thing is trying to reproduce?" Mulder asked.

"It's already reproduced," said Scully. "What it's doing is looking for hosts for its young. A body that will provide warmth and food for the growing larvae. A human body fits that bill." She paused for a moment, then added, "Mulder, if it finds a new host—"

"I know, Scully," he cut her off. "It could multiply. And then—"

Before Mulder could complete his thought, he heard Ray shouting for him.

"Agent Mulder!" he called. "A linesman spotted something down in a section of pipe!"

Chapter Nineteen

"Where is it?" Mulder demanded urgently.

"Come on, I'll show you," said Ray.

The two of them ran to the control room.

When they got there, Ray flipped through maps of the sewage system until he found the sector he was looking for.

"One of my men making a routine inspection spotted it right here," Ray said, bringing his finger down. "He phoned in his report immediately."

Mulder scanned the map. "That's the old part of the tunnel system, isn't it?" he asked. "Near where the body was found."

"Right," Ray said. "Except that this section connects with an overflow pipe that dumps excess runoff into the harbor. It comes into use only when heavy rainfall threatens to back up the system. Otherwise, no sewage goes through the pipe.

"Is the pipe big enough for the creature to fit through?" Mulder asked.

"If it came head or feet first."

"Then that's probably where the creature is," said Mulder, nodding. "It's making its way through the sewers to that pipe. It's trying to work its way back out to sea. There'll be no stopping it then if it does."

"Stopping it—from what?" Ray asked.

"Breeding," said Mulder.

"Let's go," said Ray.

They headed out of the control room and to the treatment plant parking area.

"We can take my car," Ray said. "I know the way."

Ten minutes later, they pulled up to an open manhole cover in the city street. Three sanitation workers stood by it.

"Who called me?" Ray asked as he jumped out of the car. Mulder was right behind him.

"Me," said a big, bearded man.

"You saw something down there?" Mulder asked.

"Yeah—I've never seen anything like it," the man said.

"Exactly where?" asked Ray.

"A couple of yards upstream from the overflow pipe," the man said.

Ray grabbed a flashlight from one of the men and headed for the manhole.

Mulder started to follow him.

Mulder grabbed a flashlight and started down the ladder. Ray waited for him on the catwalk at the bottom.

Ray swiftly led the way along the catwalk on the side of the eight-foot-high brick tunnel. Their flashlights played on the sewage flow below. Mulder noted that they were going upstream from where he had inspected the corpse. He was surer than ever of what had happened. He could almost see the Russian engineer's body coming through the overflow pipe and floating in the sewage until it came to rest.

"Here's the spot," Ray said. He played his light on the calm surface of the liquid waste at a point where the catwalk stopped and the tunnel made a sharp bend.

Mulder shone his flashlight on the spot. Then he sent the beam of light up the tunnel wall until it reached the opening of a large pipe.

The pipe was several feet above the sewage surface. But it was not too far for a creature with arms and hands to hoist itself into.

"That's the overflow pipe, I presume," he said to Ray.

"That's it," said Ray. "It leads to another tunnel like this one. And that one leads out to the harbor—three-quarters of a mile out."

"Is there some way to close the pipe off?" Mulder asked. He did not say aloud the rest of his thought: *If it's not already too late.*

"There's a gate that can be lowered across the opening—if the lever isn't rusted too badly," Ray said. "Wait here. I'll see what I can do."

Mulder saw the lever jutting out from the

side of the opening. He could also see that the only way to reach the lever was along a narrow concrete ledge on the side of the tunnel.

"Watch your step," Mulder cautioned.

Mulder watched as Ray worked his way along the ledge. At last he reached the lever, and Mulder let out a long breath of relief.

Ray took hold of the lever. Grunting, he pulled down. It did not budge.

"This is what I was afraid of," he shouted to Mulder. "It's rusted tight. But I think if I can pull just a little harder—"

He shifted his feet to get a firmer toehold on the ledge and pulled with all his strength.

He cried out as his feet slipped off the ledge.

Mulder watched in horror as Ray hit the sewage and went under.

A moment later, Ray's head, then his shoulders and chest, broke through the surface. Struggling to his feet in the chest high sewage, he gave Mulder a reassuring wave.

"You okay?" Mulder shouted to him.

At the same time, Mulder looked with disgust at the sewage that had splashed onto his shoes. His nose wrinkled as he smelled the foul liquid dripping on him from leaking pipes above.

"Yeah. Except I lost my glasses," Ray called out. "Maybe I can reach down and find—"

Suddenly his eyes bulged with terror.

"*Ahhhhh!*" he screamed as he went under again.

Chapter Twenty

Mulder yanked his gun from his shoulder holster. But there was no way he could get a clean shot at the creature that had pulled Ray Heintz under.

Down here, in fact, there was no way to get a clean anything—not even a clean death.

Mulder scanned the spot where Ray had disappeared. But the surface was quiet now. Quiet as a grave.

Then, yards downstream, Ray's head broke the surface.

He was screaming with pain and fear:

"Help! Get me out of here! Save—!"

Ray thrashed in the water as the creature grabbed him again.

"We need some help down here!" Mulder yelled back over his shoulder. Then he ran down the catwalk to where Ray was desperately trying to get out of the sewage.

Grabbing the safety railing with his gun hand, Mulder reached down to help Ray. Stretching, he got his hand around the foreman's wrist, and started to pull him up. Ray was about halfway out of the water when Mulder's hand slipped off the railing. Mulder watched as Ray's body splashed back into the water, followed by Mulder's gun.

As the creature pulled Ray under again, Mulder did the only thing he could do.

Though it was the last thing in the world he wanted to do.

He jumped in.

His feet hit bottom and started slipping. Throwing his arms out to the side he managed to stop himself from falling over into the muck.

Ray bobbed up again, still screaming, his arms flailing wildly. Desperately he tried to reach behind him to fight off the creature sucking at his back, its teeth digging into his flesh.

Mulder waded toward him as quickly as possible.

He grabbed Ray, and helped him over to the side of the tunnel. Ray gasped in relief. He leaned weakly against the tunnel wall.

Mulder looked at him for a split second, then shifted his gaze to the opening of the drainage pipe.

Right below the opening, a head broke the surface of the filth. A slimy, white head with its mouth covered in blood. From that mouth came wheezing sounds.

The creature reached up out of the sewage to hoist itself into the pipe.

Desperately Mulder waded toward the lever.

He jumped up and grabbed the handle just as the creature began to lift itself out of the sewage.

With all his strength, Mulder pulled at the lever. His arms felt as if they were coming out of their sockets.

By now the creature was halfway through the opening.

Then, with a squeaking, grinding sound, the lever began to move.

Slowly.

Painfully slowly.

Then faster.

Still holding on tight, Mulder fell backward into the muck as the lever came down all the way.

As he fell, he saw a massive metal gate drop down like the blade of a guillotine to close off the opening.

It hit the creature at its middle.

There was a hideous cry of pain as the gate sliced through the creature's flesh.

The gate clanged shut, and the scream vanished behind it.

Getting to his feet, Mulder saw the creature's severed lower body and legs floating in muck. As he watched, they slowly began to sink, then went under.

All that was left was a spreading stain of bright red blood.

Mulder stared at the blood as it blended with the sewage. Within seconds, every trace of it had vanished. But Mulder knew that his memories of the creature would not fade so quickly.

He turned when he heard a voice behind him, echoing the thought that was running through his head.

"Thank God it's over," Ray said.

Chapter Twenty-One

Mulder sat on a now familiar bench along the bank over the Potomac. Across the river, the dome of the Lincoln Memorial gleamed brightly in the darkness. But sightseeing was the last thing on Mulder's mind. As his eyes focused on the ground between his feet, he let the day's events play through his head.

A voice broke through his thoughts. "Is this seat taken?" Scully asked.

"No," he told her. "But I have to warn you, I may reek of the sewer."

"I'll take my chances." She sat down next to him. "You spoke to Skinner yesterday?"

After a moment, he answered. "Success in our work is imperative. Reinstatement of the X-files must be undeniable."

"That came from Skinner?" she asked, surprised.

"No. We have a friend at the FBI."

Scully paused, unable to respond. Then, changing the subject, she said, "I thought you might be interested in the lab results on the fluke larva that I pulled from the body of the Russian sailor."

"What did you find?" Mulder asked.

"I did a thorough dissection and microscopic examination. My analysis indicates a high level of reproductive and physiological cross-traiting, resulting in a sort of quasi-vertebrate human."

"Human?" Mulder asked, looking up at her.

"Yes," Scully responded. "But still capable of regeneration, like any fluke or flatworm."

"How does something like that happen?"

"Radiation," she said bluntly. "Abnormal cell development. Radical gene alteration. A shift in the natural genetic processes." She paused a moment before going on. "Nature didn't make that thing, Mulder. We did."

Reaching into her briefcase, Scully pulled out a folder and handed it to Mulder. It was full of photographs.

He leafed through them silently. The photos depicted animals and humans—all dramatically disfigured. The victims of horrible genetic mutations.

"I know these," Mulder said quietly. "They're from Chernobyl."

She nodded. "I looked into the background of that Russian ship. It was a decommissioned freighter, originally used in the disposal of material from the nuclear reactor meltdown. This creature was born in a primordial soup of radioactive waste."

Mulder stared out over the water, letting her words sink in. "They say three species disappear from the planet every day," he said. "You have to wonder how many new ones are being created."

Then Mulder stood up and strode away. Scully remained on the bench alone, watching as the lights twinkled on the silent waters of the Potomac.

Not far from Washington, the lights of New York City twinkled on the water of the Hudson River, giving the residents of New Jersey an amazing view.

Below the city, the view was not quite as impressive. Miles of sewer tunnels snaked underground, carrying water from as far away as Newark. These tunnels carried the processed waste from that city to where it could be dumped safely into the harbor.

Deep within one of these tunnels, water flowed freely through a large hole in a screen. It was through this hole that the creature had made its way into the sewer.

Suddenly, the remains of the creature rose to the surface of the water, pale and buoyant. Lifeless eyes stared up as water dripped from the walls of the tunnel.

Then the eyes blinked. Once, then again.

Slowly, the creature lifted its head. Its mouth gaped as the water carried it along. At the end of the tunnel, the creature would be deposited into the sea.

There, it would begin a new life.

And the search for a new host.

Read the next book in the
X-Files Young Adult series:

The X-Files #9:
Hungry Ghosts
by Ellen Steiber

Although night had fallen, the streets of San Francisco's Chinatown were brightly lit. Most of the shops and restaurants were open despite the late hour, and locals and tourists crowded the narrow sidewalks. Chinatown was a city within a city where rooftops curved like ancient pagodas, brass dragons edged the streetlights, and neon business signs painted the night in both Chinese and English.

On this particular night, drums and cymbals clashed out an insistent rhythm, and sparklers burned like white-gold stars against the night.

A festival dragon was winding its way through the streets. The lead dancer held the great papier-mâché dragon head aloft in his hands: silver eyes, a massive forehead with a fringe of white beard, and a bright yellow collar. Behind him a serpentine line of dancers carried the long, blue-scaled body. As the drumbeat quickened, the head of the dragon whirled and reared up as though it might actually take flight.

While nearly everyone else was involved in the festivities, one young man obviously was not. He had more important matters on his mind as he hurried away from the crowds and the brightly lit streets.

It was a chilly September night, and the young man's breath rose in a fog in front of him. Despite the cool weather, he wore only a light zippered jacket over his shirt and jeans. He walked briskly, zigzagging through the main streets, passing the fruit vendors and markets and restaurants, and finally turning onto a smaller side street. He wouldn't allow himself to run. That would be panicking. That would make him obvious. Still, he couldn't help quickening his pace as he turned into a narrow alley.

A round of firecrackers went off a short distance behind him, and he jumped, covering his ears as though it had been gunfire. Whirling, he looked behind him to the front of the alley. Four teenagers stood there, laughing hysterically. Obviously, they'd set off the firecrackers. And he—he was as easily startled as a rabbit, he thought in disgust. Then again, tonight, he had a great deal in common with animals that were prey. He checked again. No, no one was following him. But he was too shaken to maintain his former semblance of calm. He turned and ran.

He drew back in terror as he nearly collided with a figure that stepped out from behind a fire escape. The figure towered over him, at least seven feet tall, with a long face and crossed eyes. The young man bit back a cry of alarm. Then he realized it was just one of the festival mimes—a man on stilts, his face covered by a mask.

The young man shouted angrily, then pushed the oversize mime out of his way and kept running.

He crossed the alley, then raced up the back stairs of a neglected brick building. The old wooden stairway creaked with each step. He was breathing hard, desperate to get off the streets, where he knew he was vulnerable.

He reached the landing and felt his racing heart slow. His breath began to come more easily. He was home. It was all right.

And then he saw that it wasn't all right.

Chinese lettering marked his door in shiny white paint. White, he knew, was the color of mourning. As for the meaning of the lettering—he wouldn't even let himself believe that it might be true. He knew of others who'd received the same message. He also knew what had happened to them.

He reached out and touched the door, his hand trembling with trepidation. The paint was still damp, leaving white smudges across his fingertips. Which meant that whoever painted it had been here recently.

Again he turned and looked behind him. Except for a stray dog, the alley was empty.

Slowly he opened the door to the apartment. The inside was dark. The only light was the hazy glow of the streetlamps spilling in through the windows.

Moving silently, he stepped inside. Suddenly a flashlight switched on, its harsh white beam aimed directly into his eyes, blinding him, making it impossible to see the man who held it.

The stranger spoke to him in Cantonese, the language of their home. "You knew the rules. Now you pay the price."

"I told you I wanted out," the young man replied, raising his hand to shield his eyes.

"You start, you finish," the other answered.

The young man saw a metallic gleam. The man with the flashlight had drawn a knife.

But the young man had half expected this. A switchblade snapped open in his hand. In a quick strike, he slashed at the figure in front of him, cutting the man's chest and making him reel backward, dropping the light.

The young man caught his breath, wondering if he'd killed his attacker. His heart was pounding, his blood throbbing in his ears. He'd never wanted to fight. And all he wanted now was to escape.

He took another ragged breath, then felt his body begin to shake violently. His attacker wasn't the only one in the apartment.

Three masked figures stood in the shadows. They wore long robes so black that they were nearly invisible in the darkened apartment. But their faces glowed with an unearthly white light. The young man had seen these faces before in old prints in his father's books. They were the faces of ancient Chinese demons. And now they had come for him.

The watchman sat frowning at the electronic blackjack game in his hand. He was in his late twenties, tall and strong, his head closely shaved. He wore the trademark white shirt, navy tie and side-striped pants of a rental security guard. He paid no real attention to the place where he was stationed, the Bayside Funeral Home. He deliberately ignored the open casket that sat at the front of the chapel just a few yards away from him. He didn't want to look at the body, at the three red paper lanterns hanging above the casket, or even at the flowers surrounding the coffin.

This was a new assignment for him. Earlier that day his younger brother had teased him about how creepy it would be to work in a funeral home. For a split second the guard let himself think about the stories his brother had told him: the one about the corpse that sat up in its coffin, crying out the name of its murderer; and another about a ghost who haunted morgues. Well, he wasn't about to let himself be spooked.

Determinedly he returned his attention to the tiny battery-powered game of blackjack. It beeped at him as once again the computer won its hand.

Concentrating, the watchman pushed the

button for a new game and began turning over cards on the little screen. An ace and a king against the dealer's two face cards. He smiled as the machine sang out in its digital voice: "Blackjack. You win!"

He was about to hit the Start Over button when he heard a noise from another part of the funeral home. That was odd. He knew for certain that he was the only one there. He waited a moment, wondering if he'd imagined it. No, there it was again. A shuffling sound—almost as if something was being dragged across the floor.

His heart hammering, the guard turned the game off, stood up, and took out his long utility flashlight. Slowly he walked through the dark, empty chapel.

This was the first time since he had signed on with the security company that anything had happened on his shift; he could feel his adrenaline rising, his every sense heightened and alert.

As he moved into the arched hallway, suddenly there was another noise—as if something heavy was being moved or shut.

The watchman spun around and shined his flashlight along the walls of one of the receiving rooms. Nothing. He kept walking, beaming the light along the hallway and inside a room where sample coffins were displayed.

Then he went absolutely still as he heard a low rumbling. *No,* he told himself, *it couldn't be.* As he moved down the hallway to the source of the noise, he was sure he must be imagining things. Until he pushed open the painted red doors that led to the crematorium. His stomach started to churn as he realized he hadn't imagined the sound.

"Somebody in here?" he called out, his voice wavering as he pointed his flashlight in the direction of the lit oven.

Caught in his flashlight beam were three figures dressed in black robes, their faces painted white Chinese masks.

No sooner did his light catch them than they were gone—vanishing in the darkness. As if they'd never been.

Did I just imagine that? the watchman

asked himself. He felt his entire body tense as he realized that his flashlight wasn't the only light in the room. There was a strange orange glow in the darkness. And a faint sound coming from within the crematorium, as if something—or someone—was inside.

It couldn't be.

"Holy Moses . . . ," he murmured softly, starting toward the oven. The sound grew louder. He moved faster, toward the circle of orange light. Then he leaned forward, peering through the glass spy hole in the oven door, dreading what he would see.

The crematorium was lit with the dancing orange light of fire. The watchman looked more closely, squinting against the glare of the flames. And what he saw made him sick.

A young Chinese man stared back at him, his face distorted with agony, his dying screams muffled by the thick oven wall and the roar of the flames.